What's Inside?

Spacecraft

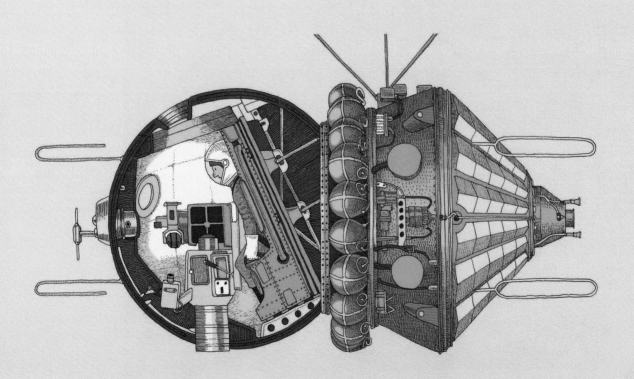

A+
Smart Apple Media

Published by Smart Apple Media, an imprint of Black Rabbit Books
P.O. Box 3263, Mankato, Minnesota 56002
www.blackrabbitbooks.com

Produced by David West ⚇ Children's Books
6 Princeton Court, 55 Felsham Road, London SW15 1AZ

Designed and illustrated by David West

Cataloging-in-Publication data is on file with the Library of Congress.
ISBN 978-1-62588-404-6
eBook ISBN 978-1-62588-433-6

Printed in China
CPSIA compliance information: DWCB16CP
010116

9 8 7 6 5 4 3 2 1

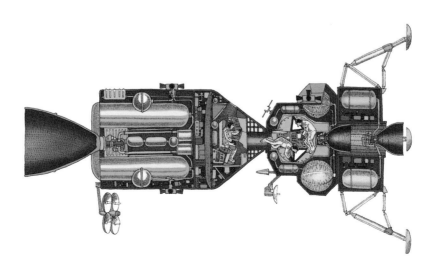

Contents

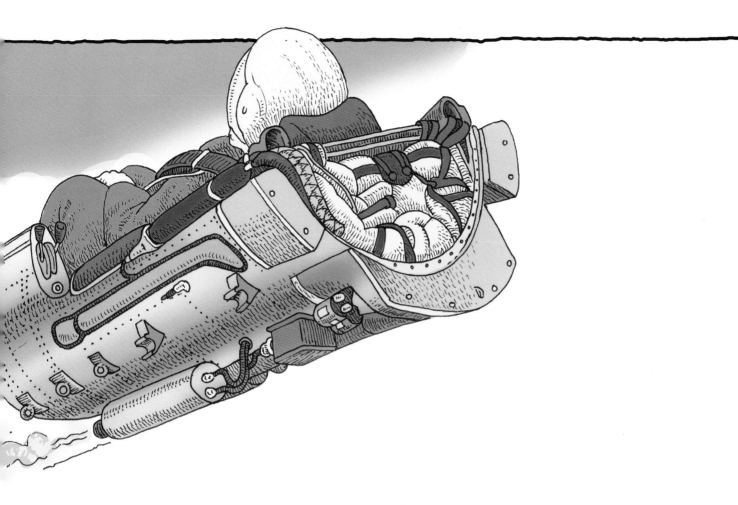

First Person in Space

In 1961, the first person flew into space. He was from Russia.

Vostok 3KA

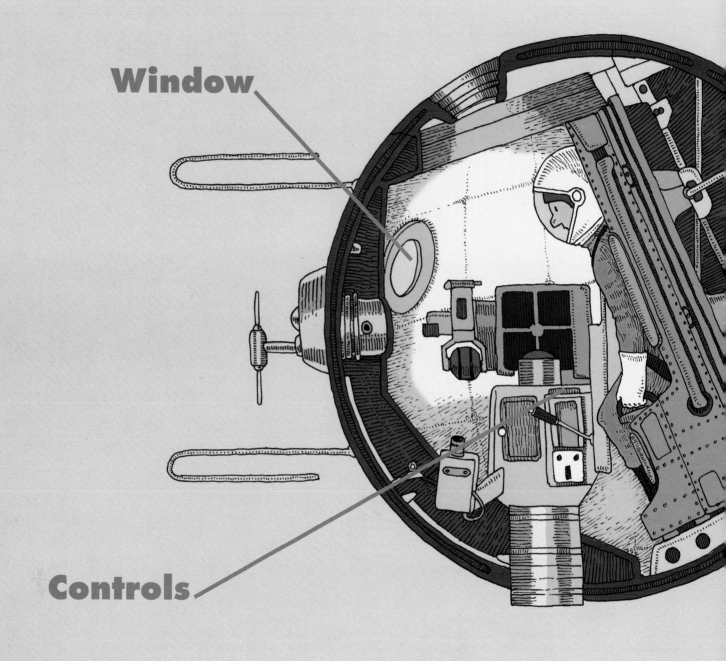

Window

Controls

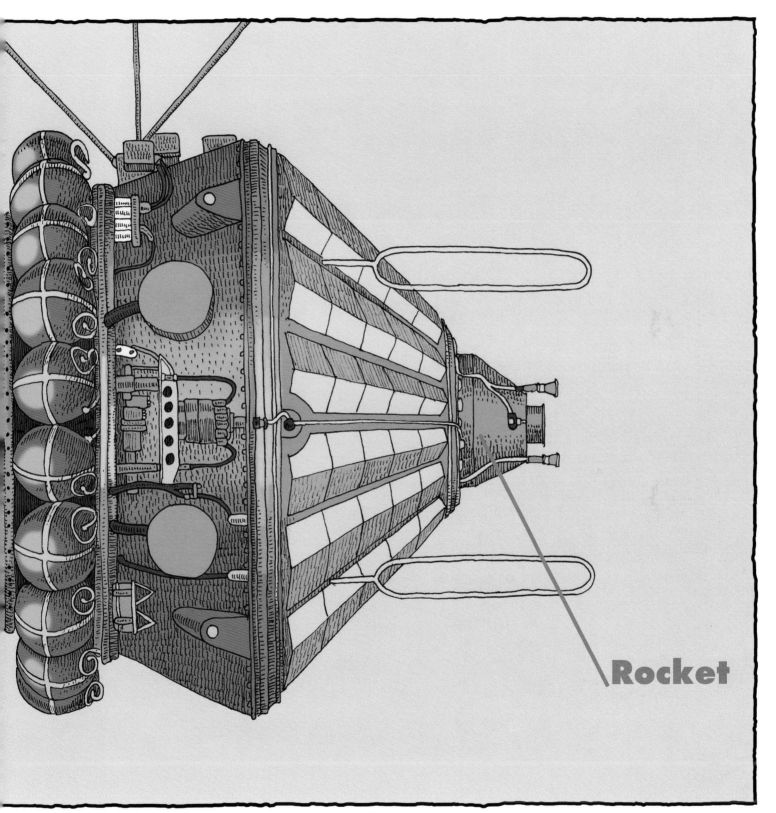

Rocket

Moon Landing

People first landed on the Moon in 1969. They were from the United States.

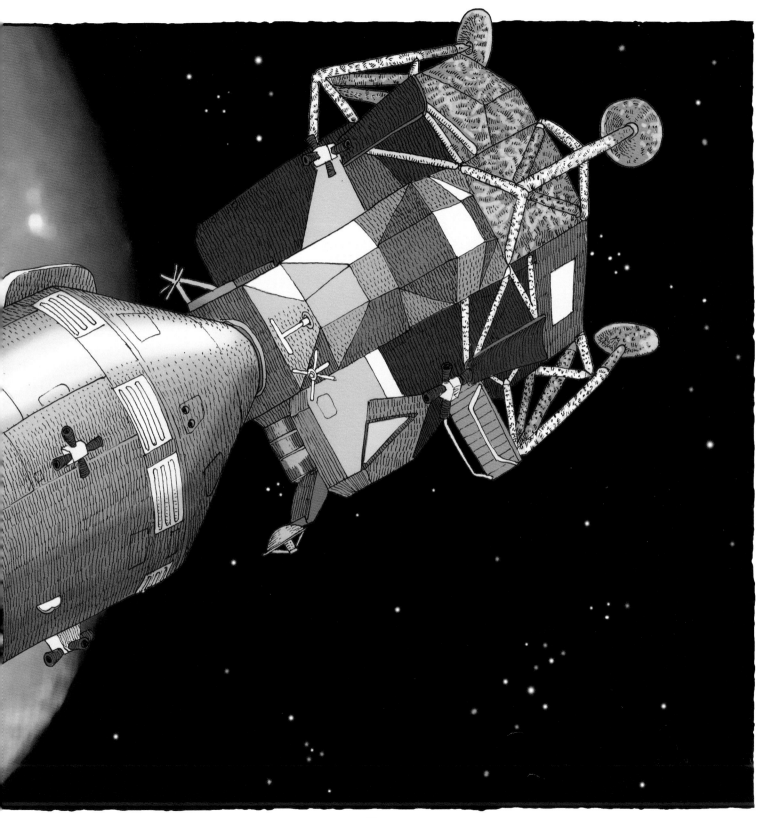

Apollo 11

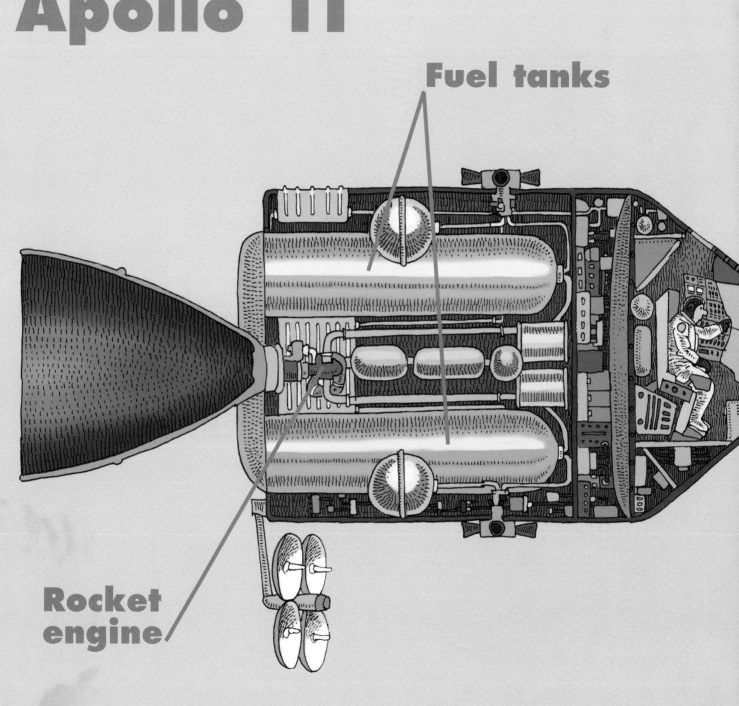

Fuel tanks

Rocket
engine

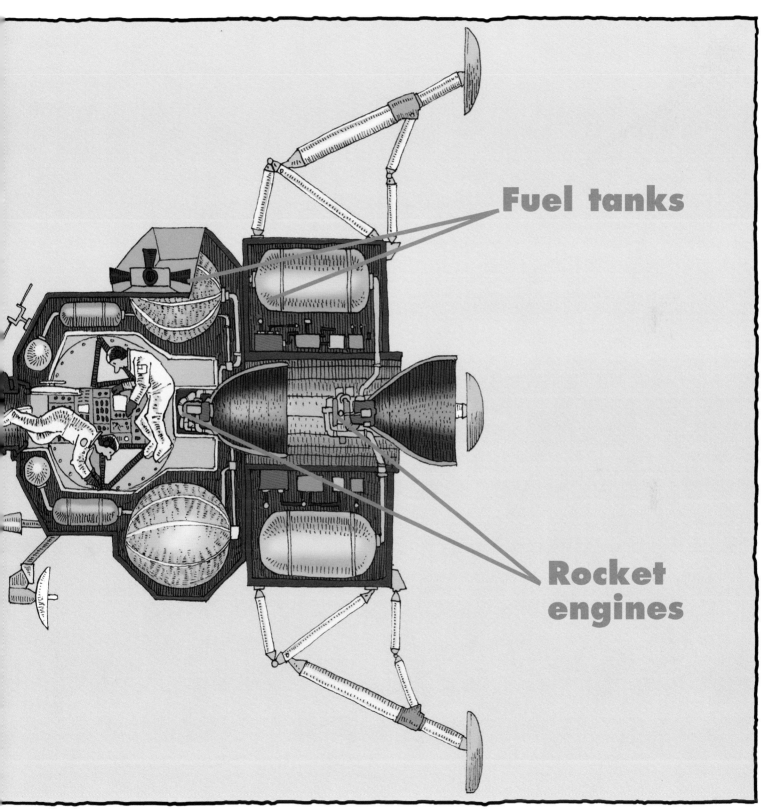

Rocket Plane

The X-15 is the world's fastest plane. It was used to help create the space shuttle.

X-15

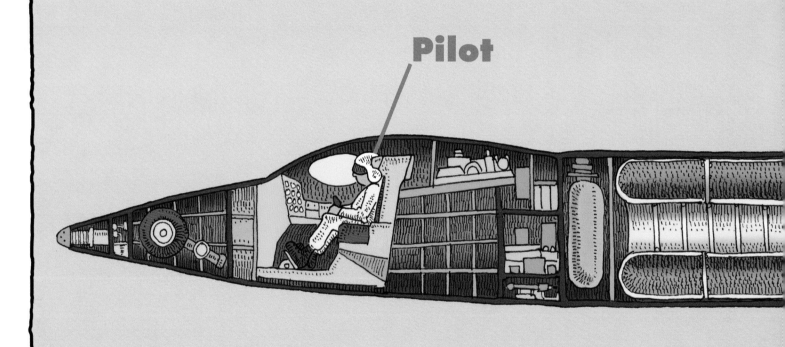

Pilot

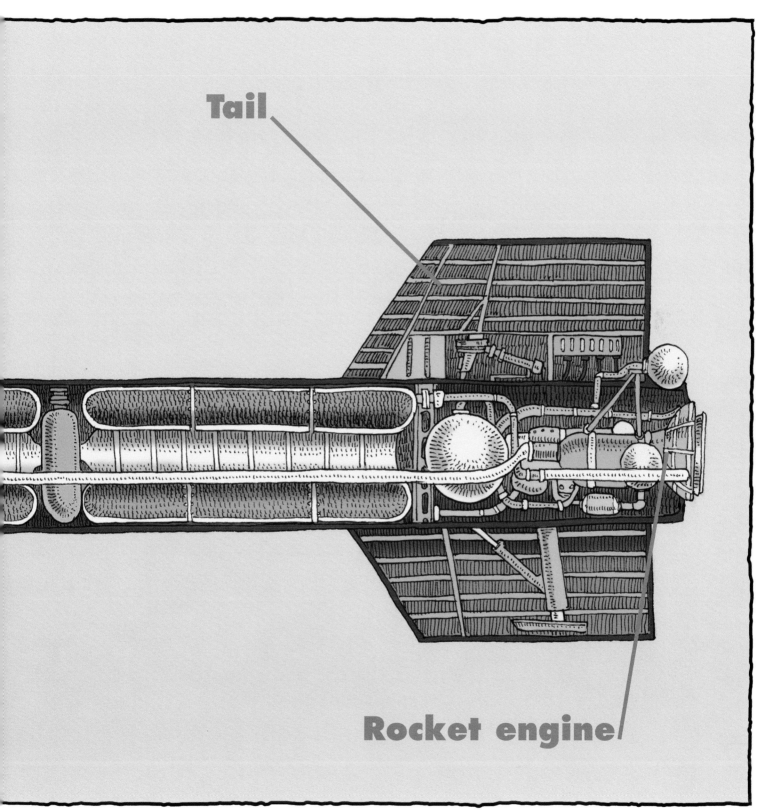

Tail

Rocket engine

The Space Shuttle

A crew flew these shuttles.
They took satellites into space.

The Orbiter

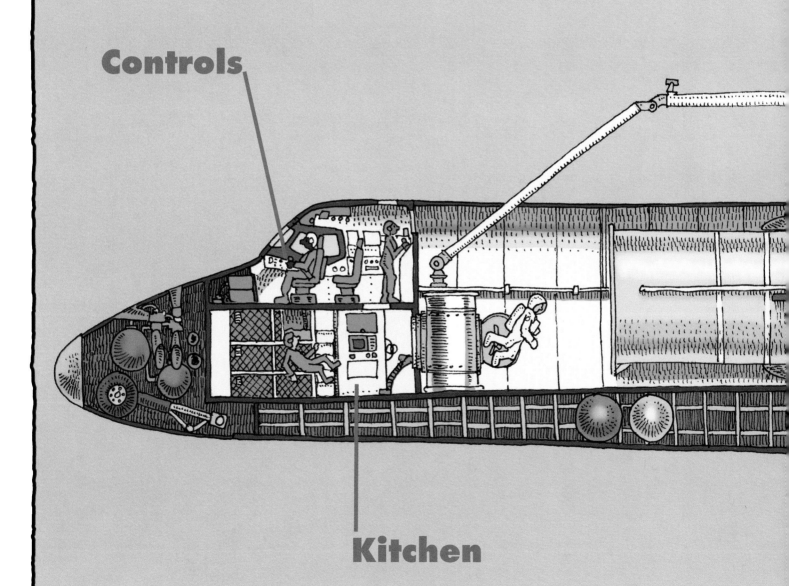

Controls

Kitchen

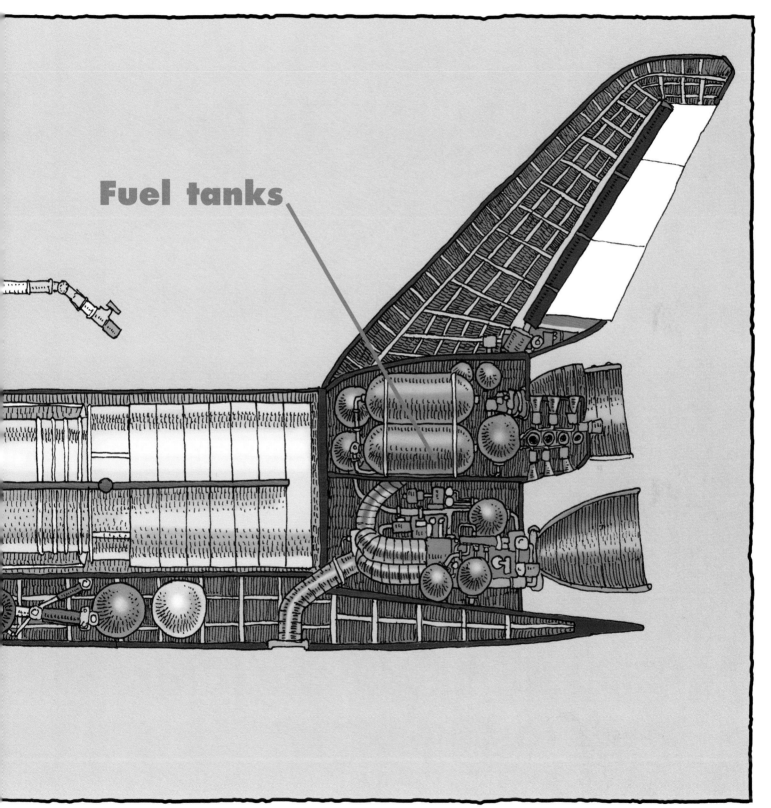

Fuel tanks

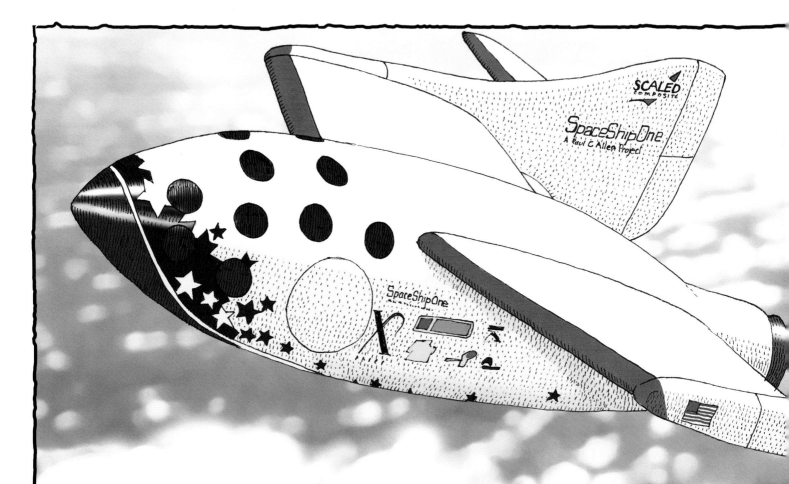

Space Plane

This plane takes off like an airplane. It may be the future of space travel!

SpaceShipOne

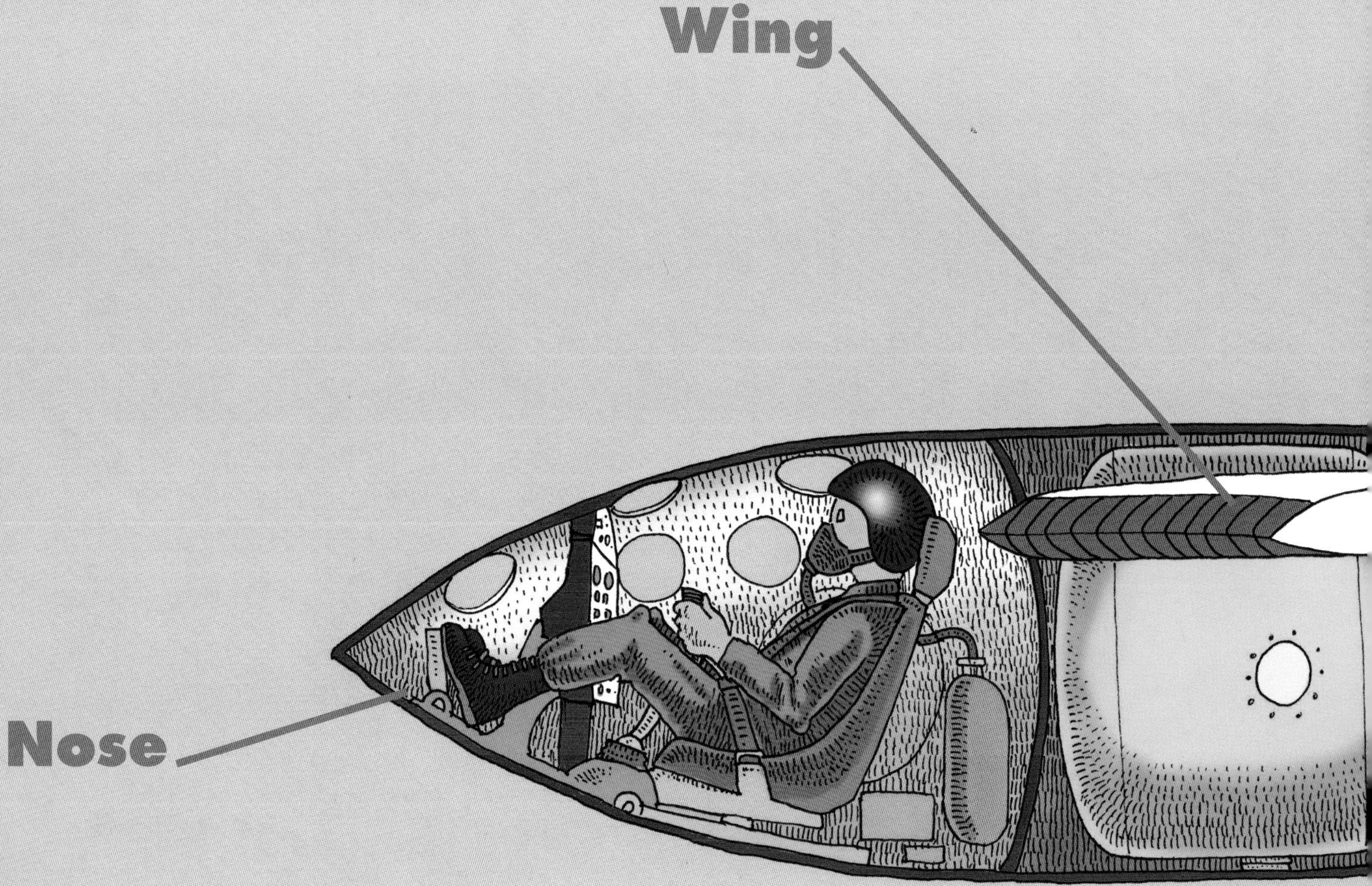

Wing

Nose

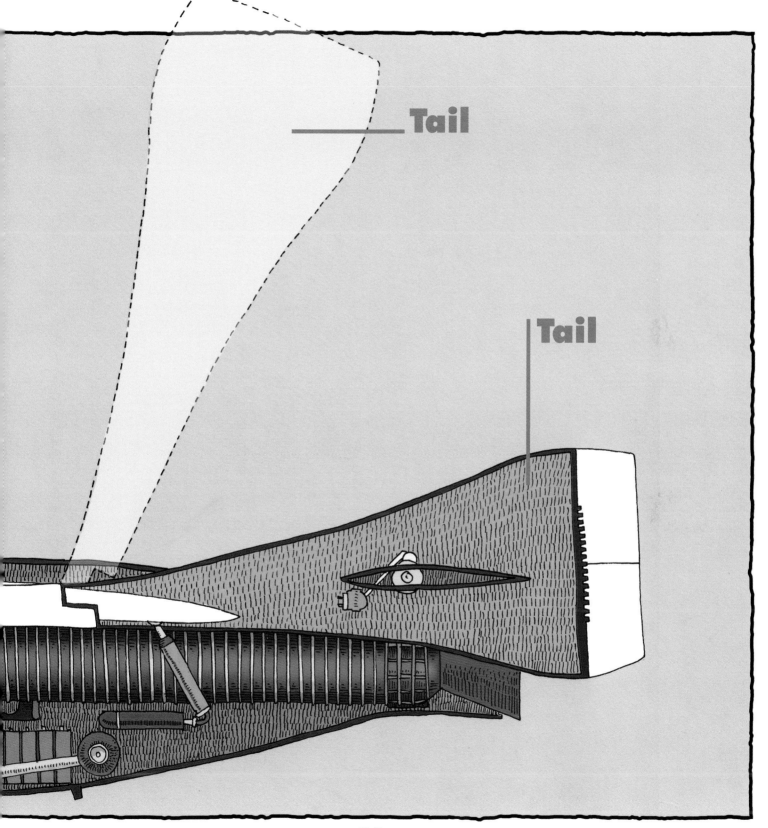

Glossary

private

Belonging to a person or group; not public

rocket

Engine powered by gases from burning fuel

Russia

Large country in Europe and Asia

satellites

Object that moves around the Earth, Moon, Sun, or planet

Index

BCPL
Baltimore County
Public Library